PETER KENT

HiddenUnder the Ground

The World Beneath Your Feet

MACDONALD YOUNG BOOKS

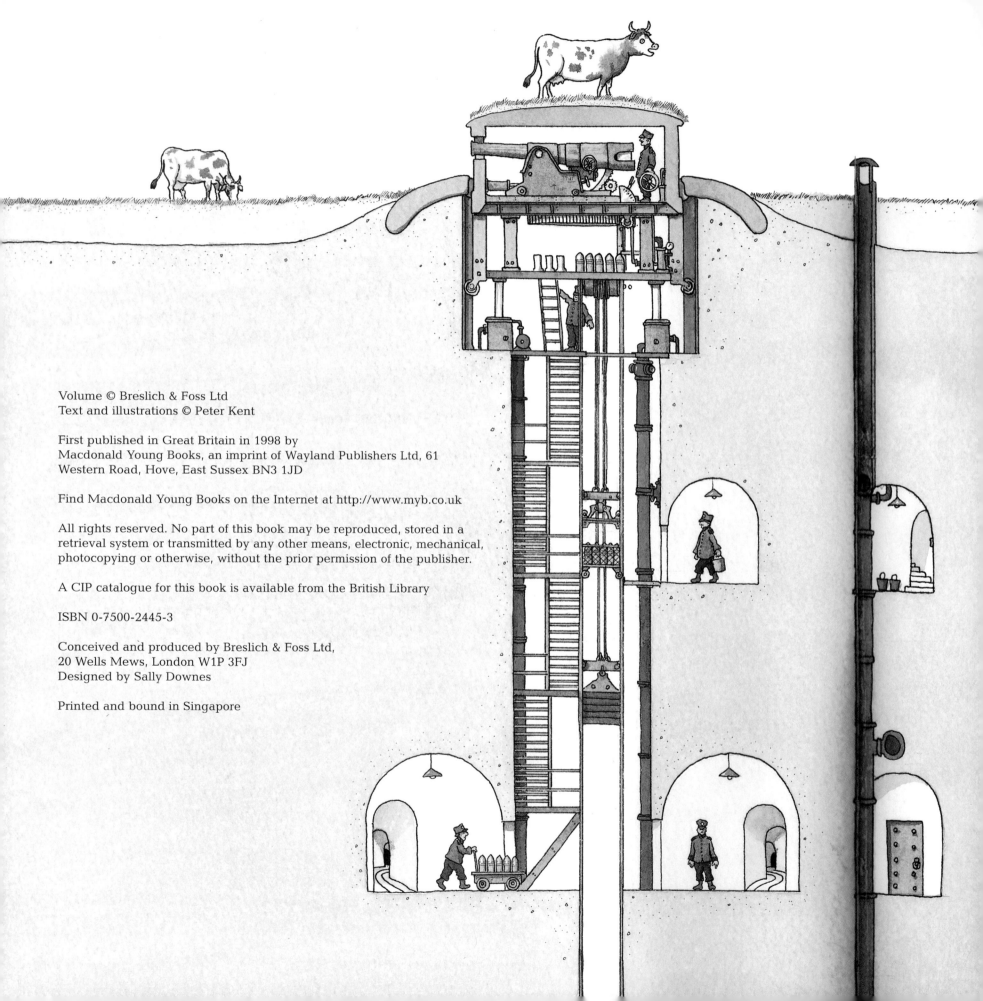

Volume © Breslich & Foss Ltd
Text and illustrations © Peter Kent

First published in Great Britain in 1998 by
Macdonald Young Books, an imprint of Wayland Publishers Ltd, 61
Western Road, Hove, East Sussex BN3 1JD

Find Macdonald Young Books on the Internet at http://www.myb.co.uk

A CIP catalogue for this book is available from the British Library

ISBN 0-7500-2445-3

Conceived and produced by Breslich & Foss Ltd,
20 Wells Mews, London W1P 3FJ
Designed by Sally Downes

Printed and bound in Singapore

CONTENTS

GOING UNDERGROUND

There are many reasons for going underground. In prehistoric times some people lived in caves, but the first reason people found to dig and tunnel underground was to reach valuable minerals. Four thousand years ago, miners in England dug down to reach the best flints, which they used to make axes and knives. The Ancient Egyptians tunnelled into rocks for gold. Since then, millions of kilometres of mine tunnels have been dug, and billions of tonnes of useful minerals have been brought to the surface.

Another reason for going underground is security. Treasure and prisoners have often been held safe in deep vaults. Underground is a good place to escape extremes of weather and the dangers of war. As guns got more powerful, soldiers copied moles and built forts underground. Once aircraft carried bombs, no one was safe above ground. During the Second World War, people took refuge from bombs in large public air-raid shelters, or in small shelters in their gardens. Governments built huge bunkers to protect their headquarters. Both Winston Churchill, Prime Minister of Britain, and Adolf Hitler, leader of Germany, had underground command centres. After the invention of nuclear weapons, governments planned shelters where a few people could survive after every living thing above ground had been destroyed.

There are many secret places underground, most of them designed for military purposes. Secret societies have often used caves to meet in. The first Christians in Rome held their services in the catacombs.

Lack of space is a good reason for going underground. In cities, buildings are so tightly packed that extra space can be gained only by digging down. All the services that keep a city going – pipes and cables for gas, electricity, water and telecommunications – run below the streets. Every day, millions of people travel in speed and comfort in trains under streets full of cars. Many of those cars are parked underground. More cities are built with underground shopping malls, and in some places it is now possible to spend a whole day shopping, working and travelling without ever coming to the surface.

SUBTERRANEAN CELEBRITIES

Hades was the god of the underworld, in Greek mythology. He lived in an underground palace with his wife, Persephone, whom he had kidnapped from above ground. All the precious metals and gems in the earth were said to belong to him.

The Minotaur was a mythical monster, half man and half bull, that lived in the labyrinth beneath the palace at Knossos in Crete. He was killed by Theseus, who found his way out of the monster's lair by following a thread that led back to the entrance.

Saint Barbara is the patron saint of miners and all underground workers. When the Channel Tunnel was dug between England and France, a statue of her was placed in a niche in the wall.

There are many legends of heroes who sleep beneath the ground waiting to emerge and save their country from danger. King Wenceslaus of Bohemia (about 903-935), the 'Good King' of the Christmas carol, is supposed to sleep beneath a rock near Prague in the Czech Republic, and King Arthur is said to rest under Glastonbury Tor, in England.

A baby was born on a train on the Bakerloo Underground, or 'tube', line in London. She was christened Thelma Ursula Beatrice Eleanor, so that her initials would be a reminder of her unusual birthplace.

Bernard Isaac lived for 11 years below the streets of New York in a railway tunnel. During the 1970s there were more than 5,000 people living underground in the city.

The eccentric 5th Duke of Portland built underground extensions to his country mansion at Welbeck, in England. They included stables, a subterranean ballroom and miles of underground roads, so that he could drive to the railway station without being seen.

Professor William Boyd-Dawkins was one of the pioneers of cave exploration. He encouraged others to explore and map the limestone caves of North Yorkshire. Boyd-Dawkins wrote the first book on the subject of potholes, *Cave Hunting*, which was published in 1874.

Germain Sommeiller was the engineer of the great Mount Cenis railway tunnel beneath the Alps, which joins France and Italy. He developed many new techniques of tunnelling and finished the work in 14 years, well ahead of the estimated 25!

THE IMAGINARY UNDERWORLD

In ancient times people had very little knowledge of what lay underground. From cave explorations they knew it was dark and cold, but people who lived near volcanoes suspected the place might be full of fire. Legends grew about a separate underworld where people went when they died that was inhabited by monsters. The Greeks believed in a gloomy kingdom of the underworld ruled by the god Hades. Other ancient peoples had similar beliefs.

Medieval artists imagined devils to be foul, dark and ugly – the opposite of angels, who were supposed to be beautiful and bright.

Lazy people were forced to engage in never-ending activity.

The worst torments were reserved for extremely wicked people.

In the centre of Hell there was supposed to be a lake of burning fire that never went out.

Satan was the ruler of Hell.

In the Middle Ages, all Christians believed that Hell lay beneath the earth. Hell was the home of Satan and a horde of devils, where the souls of wicked people went after death, to be punished for eternity. Artists in the Middle Ages often painted pictures of this imaginary place, similar to this one.

? How many kings, queens and knights can you see?

People who drank too much alcohol on earth were punished by eternal thirst.

Creatures of the Underworld

The Greeks and Romans believed that the underworld was guarded by a terrible dog with three heads called Cerberus. It stopped the living from entering and the dead from leaving.

The Egyptian god of the underworld – always shown with a jackal's head – was Anubis.

In Greek mythology, the singer Orpheus followed his wife, Eurydice down to the underworld after her death. With his music he got past Cerberus and charmed Hades into letting her go. The one condition Hades made was that Orpheus must not look back to see if Eurydice was following him. Just as they were about to leave the underworld, Orpheus looked round, and Euridice was lost for ever.

CAVES AND CAVERNS

Although we now know that the earth beneath us is not full of monsters, we still don't know very much about it. Our mines only scratch the surface, and the very deepest borehole reaches only 12 kilometres down – it is another 6,400 kilometres to the centre!

? **How many fossils can you find buried in the limestone?**

The place where a stream goes underground is called a sinkhole.

A pothole is a dry hole where a stream used to flow.

Water trickles through the limestone, dissolving it. The water evaporates, leaving a small deposit of rock on the roof of the cave. These grow downward into long spikes called stalactites.

Underground rivers form huge caverns, some of which are bigger than cathedrals. Eventually the roof of the cavern will fall in, and a long, deep gorge will be formed in the ground.

Water seeps through natural cracks in the limestone and slowly dissolves it. In some places so much is dissolved that large caves are formed.

Falling drops of water build up deposits from the floor of the cave. These are called stalagmites.

What we do know is that most of the earth consists of white-hot molten rock and metal under immense pressure, and that the core is probably made largely of iron and nickel. Scientists who study the earth and its rocks are known as geologists.

This picture shows what it is like underground in a region made up of limestone rocks.

Cave Curiosities

Some caves were lived in by people in prehistoric times. They left paintings of hunting scenes on the walls. These are the first pictures ever made by mankind, and some are 17,000 years old.

Strange white, almost transparent fish and frogs live in underground rivers where no light ever penetrates. They are blind because there is no light, so they don't need eyes.

One of the largest caves in the world is Mammoth Cave in Kentucky, in the United States. It is 6.5 kilometres long and 38 metres high.

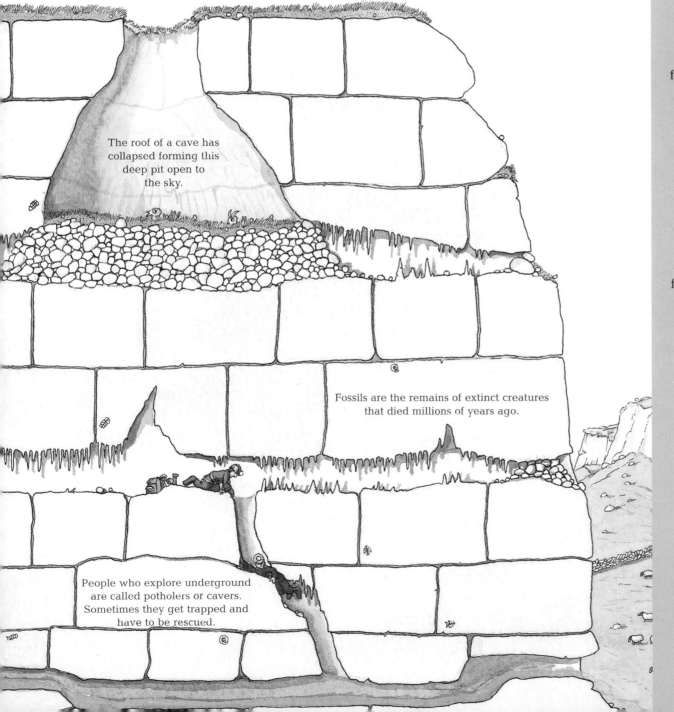

The roof of a cave has collapsed forming this deep pit open to the sky.

Fossils are the remains of extinct creatures that died millions of years ago.

People who explore underground are called potholers or cavers. Sometimes they get trapped and have to be rescued.

ANIMAL UNDERWORLD

Many animals and insects live underground for reasons of comfort and safety. A burrow in the earth keeps them dry and warm, or cool, and once they are inside, their enemies cannot reach them. Most of these animals go underground only to sleep or to escape predators, but some spend all their lives beneath the surface. There are all sorts of underground animal homes, from simple holes scraped into a bank, to complex tunnel systems that extend for hundreds of metres.

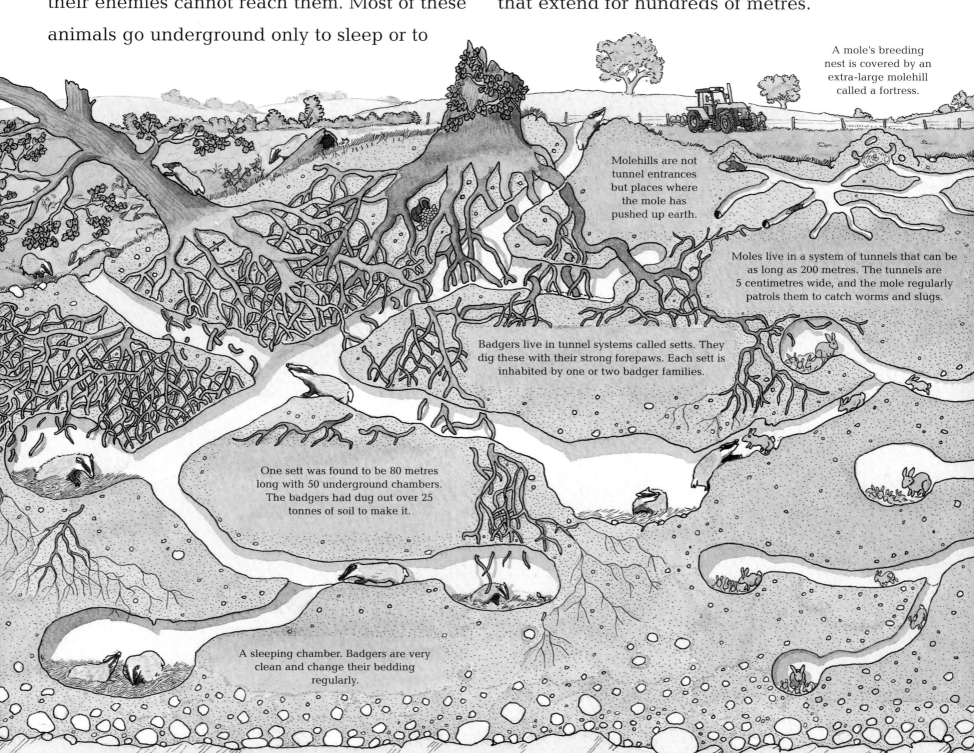

A mole's breeding nest is covered by an extra-large molehill called a fortress.

Molehills are not tunnel entrances but places where the mole has pushed up earth.

Moles live in a system of tunnels that can be as long as 200 metres. The tunnels are 5 centimetres wide, and the mole regularly patrols them to catch worms and slugs.

Badgers live in tunnel systems called setts. They dig these with their strong forepaws. Each sett is inhabited by one or two badger families.

One sett was found to be 80 metres long with 50 underground chambers. The badgers had dug out over 25 tonnes of soil to make it.

A sleeping chamber. Badgers are very clean and change their bedding regularly.

Foxes live underground only during breeding time. The female (vixen) will scrape out a den or earth under tree roots or enlarge an unused burrow as a home for her cubs.

Rabbits are very sociable creatures and live together in deep burrows called warrens. Each warren can contain hundreds of rabbits and may extend for many metres.

? Rabbits breed like . . . rabbits. How many rabbits can you find in the picture?

Rabbits breed in a nest made in a dead-end burrow or stop. The mother rabbit lines the nest with fur plucked from her chest.

Hidden Homes

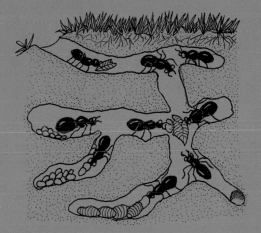

An ants' nest. Some ants' nests are like incredibly complicated miniature underground cities with millions of inhabitants.

Some spiders live in underground lairs closed by trapdoors, from which they jump out and surprise their prey.

The best burrower of all animals is the aardvark. It can dig faster than men with shovels and can finish a burrow several metres long in less than five minutes. Even baby aardvarks, only six months old, dig their own little burrows.

AN EGYPTIAN TOMB

In the past, the way the dead were buried was very important. People believed that in order for a dead person to enjoy life after death, they needed all the things they normally used when alive, like food and clothes. The Ancient Egyptian kings or pharaohs were obsessed with death and the afterlife. They began making preparations and building tombs long before they expected to die. When they died the tomb was filled with everything they needed, and their body was mummified to prevent it from decaying.

A tunnel dug by tomb robbers. They gave up before breaking in.

The sarcophagus containing a mummified body was made up of several richly decorated layers. The body inside – the mummy – had been embalmed, or preserved, and was wrapped in linen bandages.

Wall paintings tell the story of the life of the dead woman and relate stories from Egyptian religion.

A ram-headed god was put in the tomb to protect the soul of the dead woman in the underworld.

A mummified pet cat.

Canopic jars containing the intestines, stomach, lungs and liver of the dead person.

Most of these tombs were broken into and robbed of their treasures thousands of years ago. In 1922, the undisturbed tomb of King Tutankhamun was found. It was full of wonderful things. These treasures, and objects found in other tombs, give us valuable information about life in Ancient Egypt.

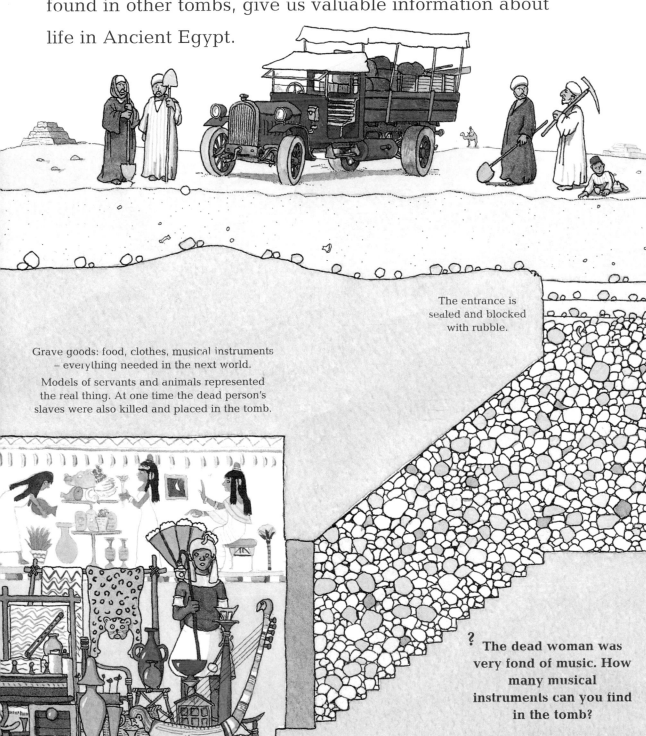

The entrance is sealed and blocked with rubble.

Grave goods: food, clothes, musical instruments – everything needed in the next world.

Models of servants and animals represented the real thing. At one time the dead person's slaves were also killed and placed in the tomb.

? The dead woman was very fond of music. How many musical instruments can you find in the tomb?

Grave Facts

In and around Rome there are systems of catacombs in which the Ancient Romans buried their dead. There are many kilometres of underground passages lined with shelves where the bodies lay. Early Christians held secret religious services in these underground cemeteries.

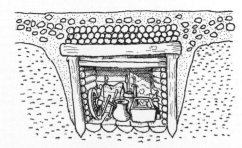

A remarkably well-preserved tomb was found in Siberia in the 1920s. The tomb had frozen completely preserving the remains of a tribal chieftain, his favourite wife and a servant.

In the nineteenth century, catacombs were built in many city cemeteries, as a way of saving space. These had modern devices, such as gas lamps, and in some places, hydraulic lifts to lower the coffins.

DUNGEONS, DEEP AND DARK

A dungeon is an underground prison: a grim, dark, damp place where light enters feebly through iron bars or high windows, or not at all. Dungeons were usually built beneath castles, but also below town halls or courts of justice.

Prisoners were kept in the basement because it was the most difficult part to escape from, and so that they would not take up valuable space in the rest of the building.

In this 17th century jail, ordinary prisoners were held together in large common cells. They wore iron chains or fetters. These weighed as much as 20 kilograms. When a prisoner was released, he had to pay the jailer a fee for taking them off.

Important prisoners had their own cells. If they had the money, they could often have good food and other comforts sent in. Some held parties to entertain their visitors.

These cells were called *oubliettes*, from the French oublier, 'to forget'. A prisoner was dropped in and, apart from the odd meal of bread and water, abandoned.

Nobody cared very much about the prisoners. They were always hungry, cold and bored, having nothing to do. The dungeons were never cleaned, and the prisoners were so filthy that many died from horrible diseases.

The jailers were known as 'turnkeys'.

The rack was a device to stretch the victim's joints.

❓ **Rats were a terrible nuisance. How many can you see in this dungeon?**

A torture chamber was a grim feature of many prisons. Torture was used to force prisoners to give information or to confess to crimes.

Prominent Prisoners

King Henry I of England (1068–1135) defeated his brother Robert, Duke of Normandy, and kept him prisoner in a dungeon. Henry hoped that Robert would soon fall ill in the unhealthy dungeon and die, but his brother lived on in prison for 28 years.

Queen Juana of Spain went mad with sorrow after the death of her husband, Philip I, in 1506. Eleven years later, her son Charles forced her to give up the throne. He then shut her in a windowless cell for 40 years until she died.

Terry Waite, assistant to the Archbishop of Canterbury, was taken hostage in the Lebanon in 1987. For five years he was kept chained in cellars. For three of those years he was alone.

MINING FOR MINERALS

For thousands of years people have dug deep in the earth for precious and useful metals. The Ancient Egyptians mined gold; the city of Athens in Ancient Greece had rich silver mines; and the Romans dug for copper, gold, iron and lead all over their empire. Coal mining became important when most of Europe's forests had been cut down for fuel. Since 1700, billions of tonnes of coal have been mined to fuel the world's transport and industry.

This horse-powered pump used three pistons to raise the water.

A winch lifted the silver ore from the mine up the main shaft.

Water flowed into the mine and had to be pumped out. This pump used a continuous chain of buckets.

Spaces where ore had been dug out were filled with waste rock.

The miners climbed up and down the shaft on ladders. Sometimes they slid down poles, or even down a leather carpet!

? How many ways of carrying rock can you see in this picture?

The mine was lit by simple oil lamps.

The miners wore a linen overall with a hood. You can see how this inspired the costume of the dwarfs in the Disney film *Snow White and the Seven Dwarfs*.

Poisonous gases were always a danger. Small birds were used as gas detectors. If the bird fell unconscious, the miners knew that dangerous gas was present.

Mining has always been a dirty and dangerous job. The Greeks and Romans used slaves, whose lives they considered unimportant. In the Middle Ages, the most skilful miners were to be found in Germany, where many machines were invented to make their work easier. This picture shows a medieval German silver mine.

More Mines

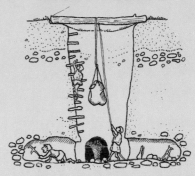

Amongst the oldest mines in the world are the flint mines at Grime's Graves, Norfolk, England. Four thousand years ago, Stone-Age men dug 11 metres deep to find the best flints to make into axes and knives.

In Poland there are vast salt mines near Kraców, with more than 1,000 kilometres of tunnels, reaching 300 metres below ground. Deep inside is a chapel, with an altar, statues and candlesticks, all carved from salt.

In 1899, English Statesman Winston Churchill escaped from a South African prison camp during the Boer War. To avoid recapture by the Boers, he hid in a coal mine, where the rats ate his candles.

This water-powered fan drew fresh air into the mine for miners to breathe.

The silver was present in rocks, which had to be brought to the surface and crushed.

The first railways were used in German mines. The rails and wheels were made of wood.

A fire was lit to get air moving through the tunnels.

Before drills and explosives were invented, miners split large rocks using wooden wedges.

Props made of wood held up the roof. Often they bent or broke under the pressure.

HOMES UNDERGROUND

It is wrong to think that only prehistoric people lived in caves, and that as soon as people could build shelters above ground they did so. Throughout history, some people have chosen to live underground. Usually the reason was that there was a shortage of the usual building materials like wood and stone. In other cases, it was simply easier to burrow into a cliff or convert a cave than to build a house on top of the ground.

This picture shows a village of caves inside a cliff on the island of Sicily. The people there were once too poor to build houses, so they moved into natural caves, which they gradually made bigger and more comfortable. A hundred years ago more than 500 people were living in this village.

? **Goats are useful animals to keep where there is not much space. How many goats can you see in this picture?**

The caves are clean, warm in winter and cool in summer.

Steps were cut into the rock so people could reach the caves.

This chimney was made from a natural crack in the rock.

The cave village had its own chapel, dedicated to Saint Jerome, who was supposed to have lived in a cave.

Living Underground

These old tombs in Egypt have been converted into living quarters for poor peasants. The houses of the dead now house the living.

Some modern houses are being built underground to conserve energy. Three metres below the surface the temperature stays constant at about 10°C. This produces a great saving on heating and cooling bills. This house is built near the sea in Florida, in the United States.

The topaz miners of Alice Springs, in Australia, have built homes underground to escape the intense heat.

THE STREET BENEATH OUR FEET

Two hundred years ago there was nothing beneath the paving of most towns except plain soil. Some towns had a few water pipes made of either wood or lead, and that was all. In modern times, an incredibly complex network of pipes and cables has been laid

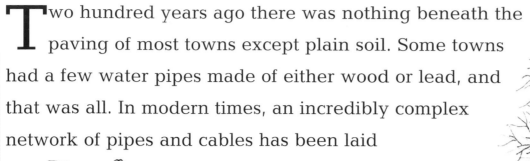

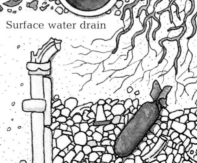

Gas main

Telephone cables

Water main for fire hydrant

Surface water drain

Electricity cables for street lighting

A layer of old rubbish laid down before the street was paved

Pipe for old hydraulic system. Water was pumped along these at high pressure and used to power cranes and lifts above ground.

Buried ruins of an ancient house

Principal water main

Old well full of rubbish

Ventilation pipe for sewer

During the Second World War millions of bombs were dropped on cities. About one in ten did not explode. Some of them are still there lurking beneath the ground. Can you find the unexploded bomb in this picture?

The oldest sewer still in use is the Great Cloaca in Rome, built over 2,000 years ago. In London, in the 1860s Joseph Bazalgette built a system of 130 kilometres of sewers, still in use today.

Small sewer

beneath the streets of every city and town. These carry water, gas, electricity, sewage and telecommunications. Without them, life in crowded towns would be impossible. They are like the veins and nerves of a person's body lying just beneath the skin.

Electricity cable

Digging a trench for fibre optic communication cables being installed.

Mending telephone and electricity cables

Surface water drain

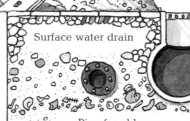

Pipe for old vacuum tube system. Many offices and shops used to be connected by a system of vacuum pipes. Messages and small packages could be put into containers and sent through the pipes.

Stalactites form on the roofs of sewers in the same way as they do in caves.

Main sewer

Rats are common in sewers. They can cause the sewer to collapse by burrowing into the old brickwork.

Small sewer

Strange Stories of the Sewers

During the Second World War, the sewers of Paris were used by members of the resistance fighting the occupying Germans. They held secret meetings and stored weapons in the tunnels.

In 1935 a 2-metre-long alligator was found in the sewers of New York. How it got there remains a mystery. Some people think it was flushed down a toilet when it was a baby and grew up in the sewers feeding on rats.

A sewer worker in Vienna, Austria found a bag containing diamonds and pearls worth thousands of pounds. Nobody could discover how they got there, and no one ever claimed them.

TRAVELLING UNDER THE GROUND

The best way to move lots of people about a city jammed with traffic is by underground railway. The first of these was built in London in 1863. It was called the Metropolitan Railway, and it was an instant success.

The trains were pulled by steam locomotives, which filled the tunnels with smoke.

This did not matter too much, as the line was only 10 metres underground and there were plenty of openings to the fresh, outside air. Very deep lines underground were impossible until new methods of tunnelling and electric trains had been invented. The first deep line opened in London in 1890. Other cities followed: the Paris Métro opened in 1900, the New York subway in 1904. Now there are 88 cities throughout the world with underground railways, and more are planned.

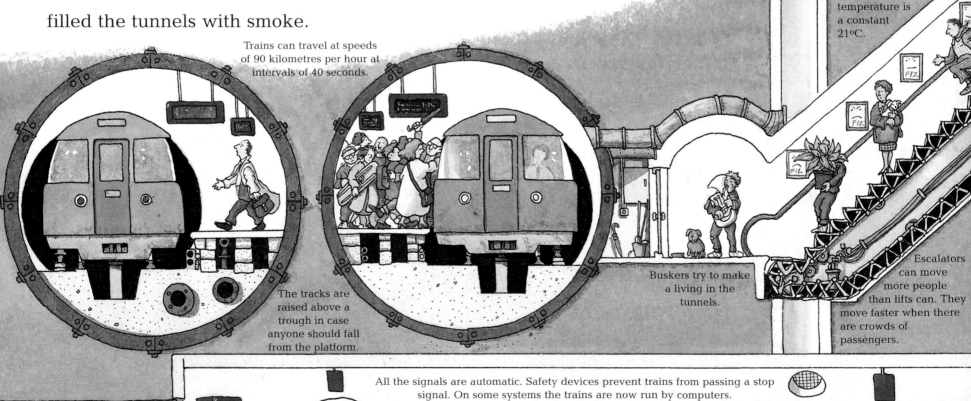

Ventilation shaft; travel on deep underground lines would be impossible without efficient ventilation. Huge fans keep the air circulating. The temperature is a constant 21ºC.

Trains can travel at speeds of 90 kilometres per hour at intervals of 40 seconds.

The tracks are raised above a trough in case anyone should fall from the platform.

Buskers try to make a living in the tunnels.

Escalators can move more people than lifts can. They move faster when there are crowds of passengers.

All the signals are automatic. Safety devices prevent trains from passing a stop signal. On some systems the trains are now run by computers.

Ticket hall

Ticket collectors have been replaced by automatic barriers.

Advertisements on escalators catch thousands of pairs of eyes a day.

There are four rails. Two carry the electric current and two carry the wheels.

? Many umbrellas are lost on the underground. How many can you see in this picture?

Underground Oddities

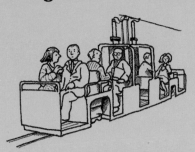

Exclusive Underground
This small electric railway in Washington D.C. is for the use of senators (members of the government) and their staff only.
It runs between their office building and the Capitol.

Explosive Underground:
The French system of frontier fortifications known as the Maginot Line had an underground railway system connecting the ammunition stores to the gun batteries.

Eccentric Underground
This carriage driven by air pressure carried mailbags beneath the streets of London. It was later replaced by a larger and longer electric postal railway.

HIDDEN ROCKETS

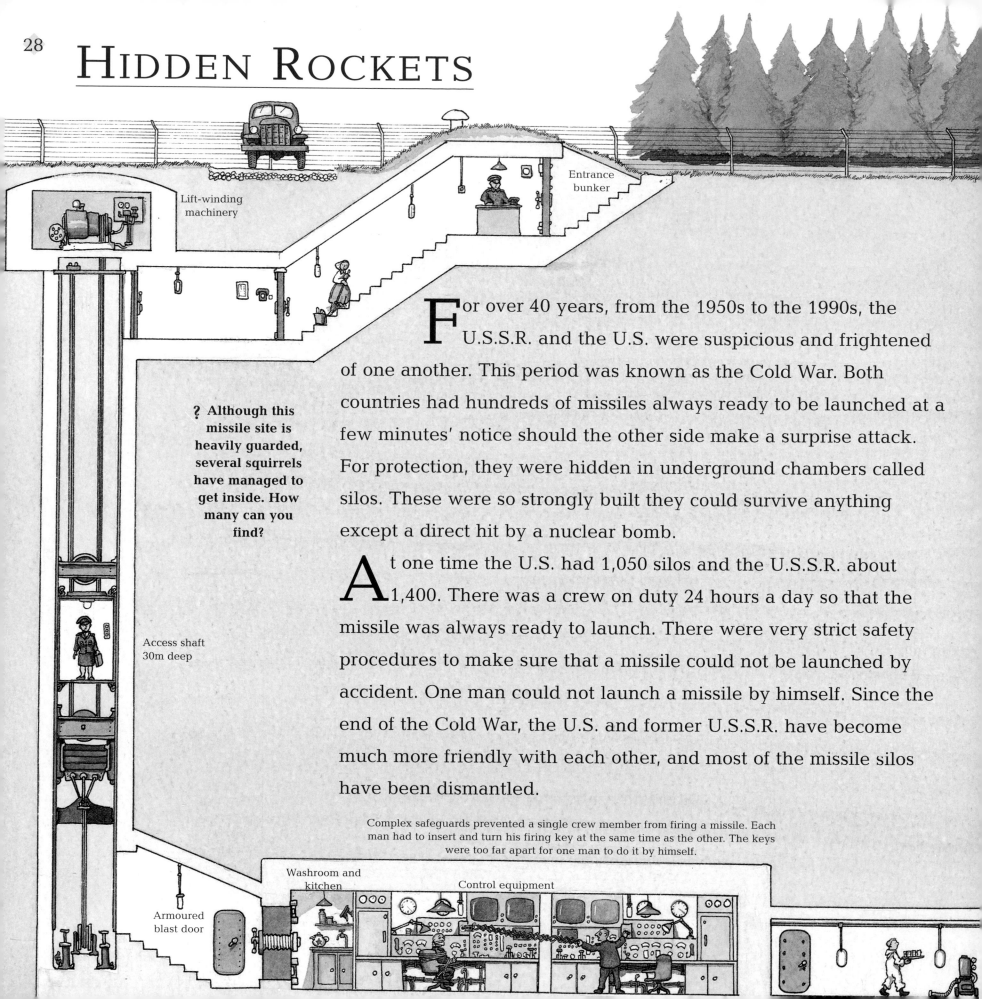

Lift-winding machinery

Entrance bunker

? Although this missile site is heavily guarded, several squirrels have managed to get inside. How many can you find?

Access shaft 30m deep

For over 40 years, from the 1950s to the 1990s, the U.S.S.R. and the U.S. were suspicious and frightened of one another. This period was known as the Cold War. Both countries had hundreds of missiles always ready to be launched at a few minutes' notice should the other side make a surprise attack. For protection, they were hidden in underground chambers called silos. These were so strongly built they could survive anything except a direct hit by a nuclear bomb.

At one time the U.S. had 1,050 silos and the U.S.S.R. about 1,400. There was a crew on duty 24 hours a day so that the missile was always ready to launch. There were very strict safety procedures to make sure that a missile could not be launched by accident. One man could not launch a missile by himself. Since the end of the Cold War, the U.S. and former U.S.S.R. have become much more friendly with each other, and most of the missile silos have been dismantled.

Complex safeguards prevented a single crew member from firing a missile. Each man had to insert and turn his firing key at the same time as the other. The keys were too far apart for one man to do it by himself.

Washroom and kitchen

Control equipment

Armoured blast door

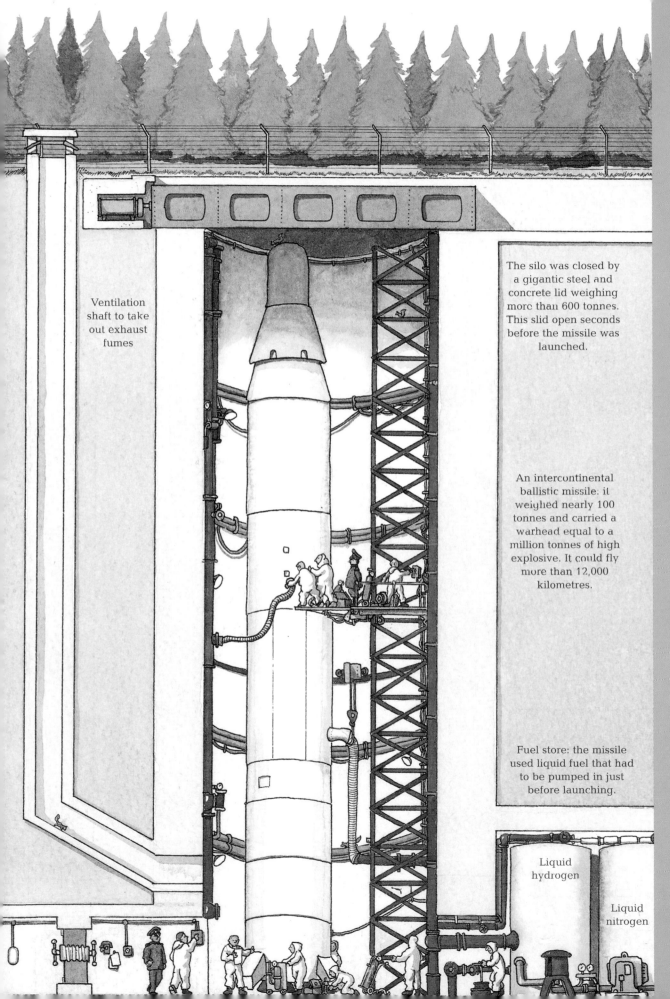

Ventilation shaft to take out exhaust fumes

The silo was closed by a gigantic steel and concrete lid weighing more than 600 tonnes. This slid open seconds before the missile was launched.

An intercontinental ballistic missile: it weighed nearly 100 tonnes and carried a warhead equal to a million tonnes of high explosive. It could fly more than 12,000 kilometres.

Fuel store: the missile used liquid fuel that had to be pumped in just before launching.

Liquid hydrogen

Liquid nitrogen

Safety in Shelters

The missiles were safe in their silos but what about the people who would be their targets? During the 1950s and 1960s governments dug deeper and deeper shelters where the top politicians and military commanders would be protected. Building shelters for everyone was ruled out because it was impossibly expensive.

The U.S. buried its command and control centre deep within a mountain in Colorado. The centre is mounted on huge springs to take the shock of a close nuclear explosion.

Some people who could afford it built shelters in their gardens. Equipped with air filters and stocks of food and water, they could be occupied for weeks.

Some governments suggested that most people could make an adequate shelter inside their house by propping doors against a wall and covering them with cushions and mattresses.

AN UNDERGROUND POWER STATION

Power stations are normally built above ground, so it may seem rather odd to go to all the trouble and expense of burying one of these huge installations. However, it is quite common.

Sometimes it is done for protection against the extreme cold, as in the north of Canada. In other places, it avoids spoiling the scenery. This hydro-electric power station in Switzerland was buried deep within a mountain because there was no room in the gorge beneath the dam. Also, it is well protected from the weather.

The principle of making electricity by water power is simple. The force of the rushing water spins the turbine, which turns a generator that makes electricity.

Electric railway: this is powered by current from the power station. All of Switzerland's railways are electric, as electricity made by water-powered generators is so cheap.

Screen to stop logs and other floating rubbish from entering the penstock.

Water inlet

Sluice gate to control the flow of water into the penstock

Overflow outlet from dam

Penstock: water flows down this pipe at a rate of 20,000 cubic metres an hour.

This dam is built of reinforced concrete. Behind it is an artificial lake, which was created by flooding a valley that contained two villages and many farms. The process took three years. The lake is 5 kilometres long and 300 metres deep. The water in it weighs over 75 million tonnes.

Water outlet

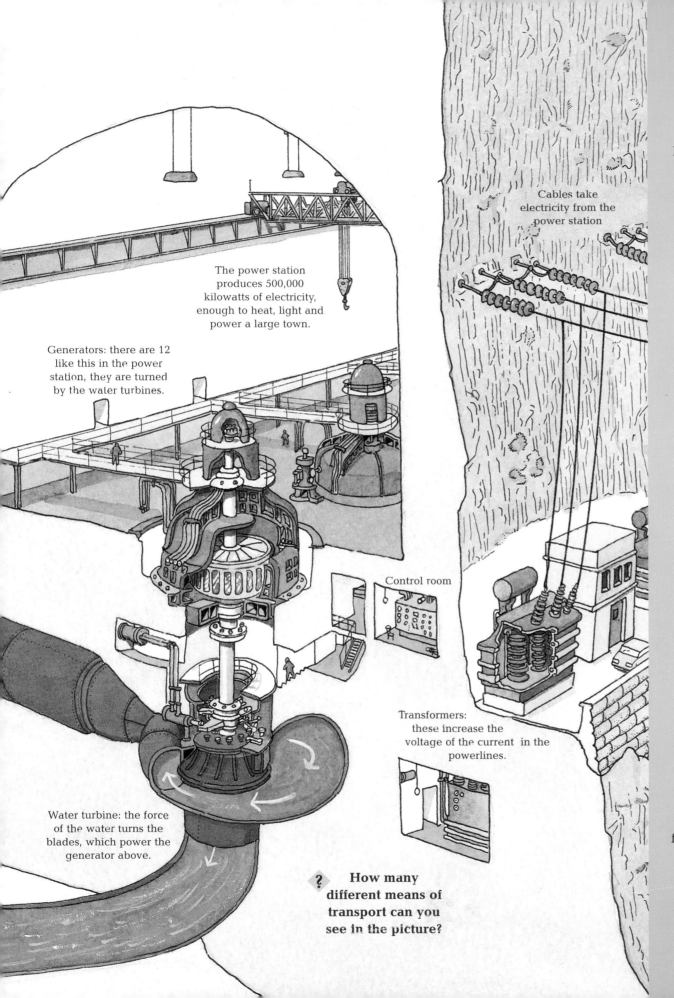

The power station produces 500,000 kilowatts of electricity, enough to heat, light and power a large town.

Generators: there are 12 like this in the power station, they are turned by the water turbines.

Cables take electricity from the power station

Control room

Transformers: these increase the voltage of the current in the powerlines.

Water turbine: the force of the water turns the blades, which power the generator above.

? **How many different means of transport can you see in the picture?**

Industrial Underground

Many underground factories have been built in wartime, when the need for safety and secrecy makes the extra cost worthwhile.

During the Second World War, 11 kilometres of underground railway tunnel in London were converted into an aircraft factory.

During the same war the Germans built a huge rocket factory beneath the Harz Mountains.

The former U.S.S.R. had an atomic bomb factory deep inside the Ural Mountains, where it was safe and secret.

TOOLS TO DIG WITH

Stone-Age men used picks made of deer antlers and shovels made from the shoulder blades of oxen.

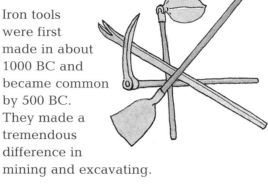

Iron tools were first made in about 1000 BC and became common by 500 BC. They made a tremendous difference in mining and excavating.

The mole's paws are the best natural diggers. A mole can move twice its own weight of 200 grams every minute.

The wheelbarrow, invented in China, was first used in Europe in about 1200. It revolutionised excavations. All of the first great canals and railways were built using simple implements such as picks, shovels and wheelbarrows.

Before explosives were invented, tunnelling in hard rock was incredibly slow. Gunpowder was used from the 1600s, dynamite and other high explosives from the 1880s. Without the power of explosives much tunnelling and mining would be impossible.

Steam shovels like this were introduced in the 1890s. Its bucket could lift 2 cubic metres at a time. It could do the work of 500 men digging with spades.

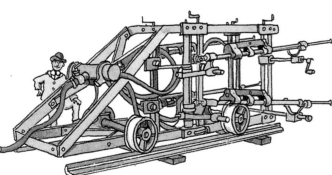

Pneumatic drills (drills powered by compressed air) were invented by Germain Sommeiller in 1858 and first used in boring the Mount Cenis railway tunnel beneath the Alps. This machine has four drills which can bore holes 2 metres deep. These are then packed with explosives.

The tunnelling shield was invented by Marc Brunel (the father of the famous engineer Isambard Brunel) in 1818 and made it possible to dig tunnels through soft soil. The roof of the tunnel was prevented from collapsing by the shield. After the miners, who worked in separate cells, had dug out a metre or so, the shield was jacked forward and the tunnel wall and roof behind lined with brick.

This machine is called a roadheader. It is very useful as it can carve out soft rock to any shape.

All coal is now cut below ground by rotary cutters like this. They are powered either by compressed air or by electricity.

Small robot tunnelling machines called moles can now dig tunnels and lay pipes beneath the streets without the need to dig trenches.

The rotary tunnel-boring machine was invented in the 1880s, but it has been fully developed only during the last 40 years. Cutting arms spin into the rock and break it up. The broken rock is passed down the tunnel on a conveyor belt. The machine is pushed forward by hydraulic rams, and the tunnel is lined with concrete. Eleven huge machines like this were used to bore the Channel Tunnel.

Glossary

Air-raid shelter a strong building to give protection against bombs

Borehole a hole drilled into the earth

Bunkers underground bombproof shelters

Catacombs underground tunnels in which the dead are buried

Cavern a very large cave

Dungeon an underground prison

Flint a kind of stone used by Stone-Age people to make tools and start fires

Generator a machine that makes electricity

Labyrinth an underground maze

Mineral metal ore obtained by mining

Missile a rocket carrying explosives

Molten solid rock or metal made liquid through heat

Mummify to preserve a dead body from decay

Ore a rock that contains valuable or useful metals

Penstock a pipe that carries water from a dam

Pot-holing the sport of exploring the deep limestone caves known as potholes

Ram a lifting or pushing machine

Reinforced concrete concrete that has been made stronger by steel buried inside

Sepulchre an underground burial place

Subterranean under the ground

Topaz a precious stone, often yellow in colour

Tube an underground railway in a deep, round tunnel like a pipe

Turbine an engine with rotating blades that is powered by water or steam

Warhead the part of a missile that contains the explosive

Answers

pages 10/11 3 Queens, 3 Kings and 4 Knights

pages 12/13 13 fossils   **pages 14/15** 69 rabbits

pages 16/17 5 musical instruments

pages 18/19 11 rats

pages 20/21 7: By dog, cart, railway truck, wheelbarrow, bucket, basket and hand.

pages 22/23 10 goats

pages 24/25 In the ruins of the ancient house

pages 26/27 5 lost umbrellas

pages 28/29 5 squirrels

pages 30/31 There are 10 means of transport: tractor, bus, car, train, bike, hang-glider, helicopter, sailing boat, canoe and walking.

  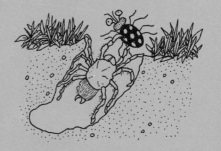